RUTH AND THE I

Charles Ashton has lived most of his life in Scotland. He has recently moved to the village where he was brought up and his two youngest children now attend the school that he went to. His books for young people include the Dragon Fire trilogy, *Jet Smoke and Dragon Fire* (shortlisted for both the Guardian Children's Fiction Award and the WH Smith Mindboggling Books Award), *Into the Spiral* and *The Shining Bridge*, as well as the novel *Billy's Drift* and another story for younger readers, *The Giant's Boot*.

Emma Chichester Clark won the Mother Goose Award for her first book, *Listen to This*. She has since illustrated a number of children's books, including the Walker titles *Cissy Lavender*, *The Minstrel and the Dragon Pup*, *Ragged Robin*, *I Never Saw a Purple Cow* and *Good Night, Stella*.

*All round the new house it was
empty and quiet.*

RUTH AND
THE BLUE HORSE

Written by
CHARLES ASHTON

Illustrated by
EMMA CHICHESTER CLARK

WALKER BOOKS
AND SUBSIDIARIES
LONDON • BOSTON • SYDNEY

For Abby

First published 1994 by Walker Books Ltd
87 Vauxhall Walk, London SE11 5HJ

This edition published 1995

2 4 6 8 10 9 7 5 3 1

Text © 1994 Charles Ashton
Illustrations © 1994 Emma Chichester Clark

This book has been typeset in Plantin.

Printed in England by Clays Ltd, St Ives plc

British Library Cataloguing in Publication Data
A catalogue record for this book is available
from the British Library.

ISBN 0-7445-3685-5

CONTENTS

When Scribble went, that left just seven cats.

CHAPTER ONE

"I don't want Scribble to go," Ruth said angrily. Her cheeks were red and her hair was tangled and her eyes felt smudgy. But the strange woman came and took Scribble away anyway.

"We can't keep kittens now," Ruth's mother said. "I'm sorry. They just grow into big cats anyway."

When they moved house, her mother explained it all to her. "We don't have goats any more," she said, "and we don't have sheep any more, and we don't have ducks or hens or geese any more, so we don't have to keep bags of grain for them in the shed any more, and that means we don't have rats any more – and that means we don't have to have so many cats any more, so the kittens must go."

Scribble was the last of last year's kittens, and when he went, that left just seven cats – Spike and Blueberry and Wattle and the four older ones. They camped in the back porch as if they wanted to let everyone know that they were not at all pleased about being taken somewhere where there were no rats in the shed. Every time you went out by the back door, fourteen lamp-like eyes would follow you, and every time you came back in, fourteen lamp-like eyes greeted you again, as if they had been fixed on the door all the time you were away.

It was very quiet in the new house. Quite often when she woke up in the morning, Ruth wondered why it was so quiet. One day her mother remarked to her father, "It's so queer, not hearing the cock crowing and the geese screaming and the goats yelling for their breakfast." And after that, when she woke up, Ruth would listen a moment to the quietness and think, *It's because they've all gone.* It felt like closing a door on a dark little room that no one would ever live in again. Sometimes, when she sang to herself, it was to forget about the dark little room.

"There's so much to do here," her mother said. "There's all the walls to paint, and the carpets to lay, and the new units to put in the kitchen, and the new porch to build at the front door, and there's flower-beds to dig and shrubs to plant, and a vegetable garden and goodness knows what else. I hope you'll help with everything – and so will Ben." Ben, as usual, was playing with his cars.

At the moment, the garden was just a flat piece of grass that ended in a steep bank down to a stony stream. All along the top of the bank there were masses of faded snowdrops, and a tree with a shiny reddy-brown trunk leaned out over the bank as if its branches were trying to reach down to the water. One of Ruth's first jobs was to make sure Ben didn't rush off over the grass and tumble down the bank into the stream.

The stream ran through a little valley which was like a sharp groove cut through the softly rumpled fields all around. On the banks of this valley the grass was rough and pale brown, with dark-green thickets of broom and gorse out of which, here and there, the odd yellow flower peeped, like stars on a cloudy night.

All round this new house it was empty and quiet, with a hill-country quietness. There were not many trees, and hardly any other houses. On soft days the air was filled with lark-song and the quiet rustling of the stream. On loud days, the wind made it difficult to stand up, especially for little Ben. The cats would watch him taking ages over getting his jacket and boots on, but they never had long to wait before they could watch him coming back in, hollering that he was cold.

Ruth didn't help as much as her mother would have liked. It was the Easter holidays, so she had plenty of time, but she preferred to wander around outside by herself. Standing at the edge of their ground, she soon picked out a lonely pine tree which she liked especially. She went out along the back track one morning and climbed the steep rabbit-paths of the mound on which the pine tree grew. A flat branch stuck out just about the level of her head, and she climbed up onto it and sat there till lunch-time. She looked all round her. There was a big black rounded hill on one side, still streaked with snow; on another side, in the distance, a gloomy grey and white mountain with dark clouds that gathered and cleared around it; on the third side, a long, low hill covered in forest – stripes of forest, green stripes and brown stripes: her father called it a plantation, not a forest. It all looked very new and strange, and Ruth wasn't sure if she liked it. Their old home had been surrounded by tall trees on three sides and a high stone wall on the fourth. Everything here was very open and large, and the breeze blew keenly against her face and ruffled her hair. "Everything's changed," she said aloud to herself. "Nothing's where it should be."

She thought her father felt the same way, though her mother seemed very excited about organizing the new house, and choosing paint and wallpaper and pot plants. Her father never knew where anything was. "Do we have a place for boots in this house?" he would ask, as Ben followed him around in his outdoor clothes and his socks, or, "Don't we have any towels any more?" Sometimes Ruth would show him where the thing was he wanted, but sometimes she would say she didn't know. After all, it was Mum who had wanted to move house, so Mum could just get on and tell Dad where she'd put everything.

"Go on, shoo, get out," her mother would tell her father. "It's time you were getting that garden sorted out or you'll be too late for this year." Ruth would sometimes go out with her father and listen to his plans for planting bushes or potatoes or making paths; but he never seemed to do much work. "We'll plant apple trees here," he said,

"We'll plant apple trees here."

waving his arms around at one end of the grass, "and in ten years' time there'll be an orchard and we'll have apple pie every night."

"With cream," Ruth put in.

"And here," her father went on, flapping his hands at a different patch of grass, "I'll put down some sheets of black polythene. They'll kill the grass and weeds and next year I'll only have to dig it over and we'll have a flower-bed all ready-made. And we'll have a rockery on the bank down to the stream."

"I wish we still had our goats," Ruth said.

"I don't have to go round repairing fences all the time any more," her father said. "That's what it means for me, not having goats. I hated repairing fences. But I do miss the goats."

Ruth climbed onto the sitting-branch.

CHAPTER TWO

It was not long before Ruth began to feel lonely. There were not many other people about, and those that she saw were always in the distance, striding purposefully off across the hummocked fields. She decided the lone pine tree would have to be her friend. Every day she went to it and sat on the soft, dry earth among its bared roots and picked at its flaking orange trunk, or when the wind was not too cold she climbed onto the sitting-branch and watched, while the tree whispered and hissed at her endlessly.

Just at the foot of the mound where the pine tree stood, the back track split into two tracks which went off round two sides of a field of pale grass. Where the track split, someone had put up a signpost. The track that led round one side of the field was marked TO SCHOOL, and the track round the other was marked TO THE SEA. The path to school went off up and over a ridge of grey-green pasture, and the path to the sea went past the gate of the field and so off towards the shadow of the striped forest.

It was in the field of pale grass that Ruth saw the blue horse. She was sitting on her watching-branch one grey afternoon when she felt light about her and realized the sun had suddenly come out. It seemed a long time since she had seen the sun. Ahead of her, dark clouds hung low over the striped forest, but the sun was making them glow grey-blue, like rain-washed slate. The pale field became like a mist of gold and slate-blue shadow. Out of this mist the blue horse appeared.

For a long time Ruth stared at it. She did not immediately think its colour was strange – the first thing she thought strange was that she had never noticed a horse in that field before. Then she started thinking that this horse couldn't really be blue but must just look blue because of the sunlight and the dark clouds. But the horse stayed blue however much she stared, and when the sun went behind the clouds and everything was dull again, it was as blue as ever – not blue like slate, but the deep blue of violets growing in a grassy bank – while its mane and its tail swirled like pale mist round its head and its hind legs. It was trotting quietly up and down the field, as graceful as a deer.

Ruth slipped quietly off her branch and tiptoed down the mound to the track. She didn't want to disturb the beautiful creature. But the blue horse showed no sign of being disturbed, and came running straight towards her. There were gorse bushes and thorn trees round most of the field, and Ruth went along the track to the gate so that she could see the horse properly. It trotted along on the other side of the hedge, and when she came to the gate it was already standing there.

It was the colour of the evening sky, with its pale mane falling like a cataract over its curved neck. Its eyes and its hooves glowed faintly – its eyes dark amber-yellow, its hooves like coals in the embers of a fire. Ruth put her hand on a bar of the gate, and the blue horse bent its head and nuzzled her fingers with its soft nose.

"Who are you?" she whispered. "What are you?" She half-expected the strange

Ruth put her hand on a bar of the gate.

horse to speak – after all, a speaking horse would be no stranger than a blue horse – but it made no sound. After a little while, it moved round until it was standing alongside the gate. There could be no doubt what it wanted: it wanted Ruth to climb onto its back.

"Where would you take me?" she whispered. "Down to the sea?" She climbed up onto the first bar of the gate. She gazed at the silky blue hair on the creature's back, and gently stroked it. She climbed onto the second bar.

Then suddenly she jumped back down onto the ground again. The horse didn't flinch, it remained standing by the gate. "Not yet," Ruth murmured. "I will one day – one day soon." She wasn't scared to ride the blue horse. It was more that she didn't feel ready quite yet.

As if it understood her, the horse turned and trotted off across the field. The evening had suddenly come on. The sunlight must have been the sun setting. Over towards the edge of the forest, the blue horse melted into the shadows, but for a moment longer Ruth could see its hooves glowing like red coals in the twilight.

Ruth ran to the house and burst breathlessly indoors so suddenly that she caused fourteen cats' eyes to blink, once, as she rushed through the porch. "There's a blue horse, out there in the field!" she exclaimed as soon as she got into the kitchen.

"Supper's ready," her mother said. "Can you get the plates out of the cupboard, please. Dad cooked the supper but he never remembers to get the plates out."

Her father's head was half in the oven. He pulled it out, turning a red and steaming face to her. "Where's this blue horse?" he asked.

"It's over in the field by the back track," Ruth answered.

"Someone's put a signpost up there," her father said, wiping his face with a cloth. "It says TO THE SEA and TO SCHOOL. I suppose it must have been the people who lived here before. I like their sense of humour."

Through in the living-room, Ben started screaming and banging something. "Go and see what he wants, Ruth, there's a love," her mother said.

A tyre had come off Ben's favourite red car and he couldn't get it on again, so he was hacking away at the coffee table with the bare wheel. Ruth fixed the tyre and then told Ben about the blue horse.

He listened, holding his repaired car in his hand, then, when Ruth had finished speaking, started pushing it about the floor again. "Vroom," he said. "My car's a blue horse. Vroom."

Ruth sighed and went back through to the kitchen. By the time supper had been served she didn't feel like talking about the blue horse any more, and no one asked her about it.

"We have apple pie every time Dad cooks anyway," she remarked, "even though we don't have any apple trees yet."

"Don't you like it?" her father said.

"No cream," Ruth replied.

The blue horse put its head over the gate.

CHAPTER THREE

"Can I have two sugar lumps?" Ruth asked her mother next morning.

"What do you want with sugar lumps?" her mother said.

"They're not for me, they're for the blue horse."

"I'll give you one," her mother said. "But I don't like you sucking sugar lumps. They're bad for your teeth."

Ruth went out, and as soon as she got to the gate, the blue horse was running over towards her, vivid as indigo. In the morning light its hooves didn't glow, but they had a deep reddish tinge to them as though they were only waiting for the darkness.

Ruth took out her sugar lump, and the blue horse put its head over the gate. Ruth held the sugar lump up to it in her palm. The blue horse brushed its silky nose across her wrists, and then across her fingertips, but it didn't take the sugar lump.

"Look, it's sugar," Ruth said, trying to position her hand under the blue horse's mouth. "It's for you."

But the horse lifted its head and blew sharply out through its nostrils. Then it backed away into the field.

"Hey, don't you know what sugar is," said Ruth. "It's lovely. It's sweet. Look." She licked the lump, then closed her eyes and smiled and said, "Mmmm. Delicious."

But the blue horse stood where it was and didn't come forward.

"Come on," Ruth coaxed. "You're so beautiful. Can I come into your field?" And the blue horse seemed to bow its head, ever so slightly, as if to say yes.

"I think you can understand me – I really do," Ruth said. She climbed another bar and swung her leg over the gate. The blue horse didn't move. She jumped down into the field and went carefully over to the horse, holding out her hand. It didn't move when she came near, but when she held the sugar lump under its nose again it did just as it had before, tossing its head and stepping backward.

"You're very strange," Ruth said. "Look, I'll put it on the gate for you." She went back and balanced the white cube on the top bar. It was a round bar and she had to position the lump carefully so that it didn't fall off. Then she stepped back and waited.

Presently the blue horse stepped forward. It came to the gate and seemed to sniff carefully along the bar. When its nose came to the lump of sugar it gave a sudden, very deliberate nudge, pushing the lump off into a puddle on the edge of the track.

"Well," Ruth exclaimed, "you're clever – aren't you? You meant to do that, didn't you? You know what sugar is but you just don't like it, do you?"

The blue horse turned and came back over to her. This time it didn't stand facing her but came alongside her so that its shoulder was just beside hers.

"You do want me to get up onto your back, don't you?" Ruth said. "Oh – maybe I would if I could, but you're so high."

Immediately the blue horse whisked round until it was standing alongside the gate, as it had been the night before.

"You do," Ruth breathed in wonder. "You understand every word I say. And you *do*

Ruth climbed up till she was level with the horse's back.

want me to get on your back. Let's see." She eased herself behind the horse and climbed up till she was sitting on the top bar, level with the horse's back. All she had to do was swing her leg over and she would be there.

She looked down at the fine hair on the beast's shoulders, like a hillock of sleek blue grass. It looked as though it had never had anyone on it before. It was clean, downy, untouched. "No," Ruth whispered, "I can't. Not yet. Not yet." She swung herself over the gate onto the ground outside the field. The sugar lump had dissolved into a tiny, sad, grey-white heap in the middle of the puddle. Ruth left it and went thoughtfully back to the house.

Every day after that – sometimes two or three times a day – she went to the field of the blue horse. Whatever it had thought of her sugar, she thought of it as her friend now. Sometimes it was there, and sometimes it wasn't. But whenever it was, it would come running over to her.

"You're really my best friend, you know," she told it. "I could sit on my tree, but I couldn't really talk to it. I can talk to you, but I won't sit on you. And I know you can understand me, but I wish you would talk to me. Maybe – maybe, if you would talk to me, you would tell me where you want to take me on your back. I'd like it to be the sea, but it wouldn't really matter. If you told me maybe I'd get on." It was obvious to Ruth that the blue horse would want to take her somewhere. It didn't seem at all the sort of horse that would be content simply to run round and round a field.

"Where do you go when you're not here?" Ruth asked it. "How do you get out of the field?" But the blue horse just looked at her calmly with its deep lilac-shadowed yellow eyes.

The Easter holidays drew to an end. "I'll be going to my new school," Ruth told the blue horse one evening. "In just two more days."

She held a primrose up to its chin. "Do you like butter?" she said. "Look, I do." She held the primrose under her own chin and pointed. "See? The yellow light on my chin? It means I like butter. I don't suppose you do though." The blue horse seemed very interested in the primrose, though not in discussing butter. It seemed to sniff each of the flower's five petals in turn, very gently.

"Eat it if you like," Ruth said, but the blue horse just went on sniffing.

"Come on," said Ruth, suddenly turning and running off over the grass. "Come and get it!" The horse followed her, and for half an hour the pair of them ran up and down the field. The blue horse kept close behind her, its nose at her shoulder and its pale mane streaming back like smoke. Ruth didn't know if it wanted to go on sniffing the primrose or if it was simply being playful, but it didn't matter. She thought they were the most wonderful moments of her life – running in the quiet evening air with the mysterious creature running so close.

She stopped, panting and laughing, and realized she had dropped her flower. "I like you, Blue," she said breathlessly. The blue horse stood silently while she got her breath back.

"I like you, Blue," she said again, more thoughtfully. "But I do wish you'd talk to me."

*Ruth and Martin went about
everywhere together.*

CHAPTER FOUR

It was a small school. Ruth didn't get to it by following the track marked TO SCHOOL, but by going in the opposite direction, by the front track and then the tarred road, to meet the school bus. There were fifteen other children in the class, quiet, shy country children like herself.

One of them wasn't so shy. "I'm Martin," he said. He had dark curly hair and rosy cheeks and he smiled at everything. "Our goat's just had kids," he said. "My dad's going to keep them for the freezer."

Ruth didn't like to think of the goat-kids being killed, but she did like Martin, and very soon they were going about everywhere together. Martin didn't have any brothers or sisters, and he was often quite rude about very small children, which Ruth liked because Ben so often annoyed her. "Cats caterwauling," Martin remarked when they heard the children at Ben's playgroup in the spare classroom singing "Twinkle, Twinkle, Little Star".

"Kittens," Ruth said reprovingly, though she couldn't help agreeing.

Martin's shoes were always muddy and the teacher was always grumbling about them. "I can't help it," he told the teacher. "My dad says that Adam and Eve were made out of mud, so it should be good enough for everyone else."

That made the teacher laugh. "We'll see what your mother has to say about that when she comes in to clean the school," she said.

Just across from the school, a straight,

narrow road led up between two grass fields to a small group of houses. Martin lived in one of these, and behind the house there was a space of churned-up grass with a muddy pond in the middle and some tumbledown wooden sheds at the top end, all surrounded by a fence of half-rotted wooden boards and old bed-frames. In the sheds lived Martin's twenty-four hens, thirteen ducks, two pigs, two goats, six geese and one pony. It reminded Ruth a little of her old home, except that it was much muddier and scrappier.

The pony was called Fuzz. Her coat was patches of chocolate-brown fur and mud-brown hair and grey flaky skin. She was very small and very gentle. When she was let out of her stall – or had pushed her way out – she would stand by the back door of the house, and when she got a chance she would push her way into the kitchen and raid the bread-bin.

One of the grass fields was over the fence from the muddy space. When Fuzz was let out into it, she would go round to the fence at the roadside and push her way through it and stand in the middle of the narrow road up from the school. People who didn't know her would stop their cars and honk their horns and wait for her to move, but she never did. People who knew her would drive slowly up against her and push her out of the way with their cars – that was the only way to move her.

When Ruth got to know Martin better – which didn't take long – she would sometimes go to his house after school instead of getting the school bus home. Then her father would pick her up as he came through the village on his way home from work.

Once when she had been fetching her school-bag from the house, Ruth saw Martin's father leaning against the car and talking to her father through the open window. Martin's father grinned at her as she got in. "Red sky at night, shepherd's delight," he said with a mysterious wink towards the sky, which was indeed edged with red clouds.

"That man's totally cracked," her father remarked as they drove off. "I like him though."

"Martin says he's a weather-watcher," Ruth said.

"What's that?"

"I don't know, he just stands by the fence and Martin says he's watching the weather."

Her father laughed. "That's the best excuse for doing nothing that I've ever heard," he said.

"Martin says he's always right, even when the forecast on the telly's wrong."

"I can believe that," her father said.

Martin's mother seemed to have various jobs, apart from being the school cleaner, but his father was always at home. He always looked a bit muddy and crumpled and he always wore boots and a black waistcoat and a black hat with a broad brim, underneath which his black-and-grey hair straggled out like pondweed. His face was always dark with hair, but never enough to call a beard, and he always had a brown cigarette hanging out of the corner of his mouth. "Hello, young people," he always said when Martin and Ruth came back from school, taking his hat off and bowing to Ruth. But that, and his remark about the red sky, was all Ruth had ever heard him say.

She helped Martin to feed the ducks,

though she kept away when the geese were around, as they didn't seem very friendly. She liked to throw bits of stale crust onto the water of the pond and watch the ducks paddle frantically out to them and scoop them up with their flat beaks just as they were starting to sink. One of the pigs was friendly and would stand with its forefeet up on a rail of the fence and rub noses with her, which tickled and made her sneeze. But the goats lay at the back of their stall with their forelegs tucked under them, staring snootily and chewing.

Fuzz would let anyone ride her, even the little white goat-kids, which would stand on her back, balancing like circus performers, while she ran round the field.

"Coming for a ride?" Martin called to Ruth.

Fuzz was so small that Martin could jump

Fuzz was very small and very gentle.

onto her back quite easily. He rode her round the field, shouting at her all the time to go faster, though she never went beyond a gentle trot. He brought her back, laughing, to where Ruth stood watching and tumbled off onto the grass. "Do you want a go?" he said.

"All right," said Ruth. "But I can't jump up like you can."

"Hang on a minute," Martin said. He scrambled over one of the bed-frames into the muddy paddock and went running up towards the sheds. Fuzz nuzzled at Ruth's pocket until she remembered that she had a Malteser in it. "It's all grey and hairy," she said, but Fuzz didn't seem to mind.

In a minute Martin returned with a bucket, which he upended. Ruth stood on it and scrambled onto Fuzz's thick-smelling, dusty back, pulling herself up by the rough hair of her mane. It was as well Fuzz was so patient.

"Hang on with your knees," Martin advised, but Ruth couldn't, because Fuzz's back was so broad her legs were sticking straight out to the sides. She twined her fingers into Fuzz's mane and Martin slapped the pony's side and they bumped away.

Her teeth knocked together and her tongue crunched painfully. She got a glimpse of Martin's house, bumping up and down, up and down, and then a glimpse of the sheds and Martin's father leaning on his fence, bump, bump, up and down. She shut her eyes and felt glad it was only Fuzz and not the blue horse. Riding wasn't easy, and she would have felt terrible if she'd got onto the blue horse's back and then bounced up and down like a sack of potatoes. She was sure Martin hadn't bounced like this when he was riding Fuzz. She would have to practise riding on Fuzz until she was a good rider, and then she'd have a ride on the blue horse. But for the moment she just wished that Fuzz would stop bouncing her.

Fuzz stopped. Not where Martin was, but where she felt like stopping, which was beside a gorse bush. Ruth slipped off backwards into the bush, which was exceedingly prickly but at least stopped her crashing onto the hard ground. Fuzz wouldn't move when Ruth tried to scramble out, and eventually she had to wriggle feet-first under the pony's belly.

Martin slowly climbed onto the gate.

CHAPTER FIVE

The road from the school to Martin's house continued on up the hill as a track. "That's the way to your house," Martin said.

"Is it?" Ruth said. "That must be the track that's marked TO SCHOOL. I always go by bus though."

"I'll take you home that way some time," Martin said.

Ruth still liked to see the blue horse, and she would still greet it – "Hello, Blue, where have you been running today?" – but she didn't spend time with it any more. The pine tree had been her friend till she met the blue horse, and the blue horse had been her friend till she met Martin. She still liked the tree and the horse, but they couldn't talk, and she liked to have a friend she could talk to.

One day she and Martin arranged to walk home together to her house. They set off on the track up the long hill, stopping at Martin's house just long enough for Martin to leave his school-bag. Then they took it in turns to carry Ruth's. It was three-quarters of an hour before Ruth at last saw her pine tree appearing over the top of the last grassy ridge. She explained to Martin how she had used to sit on the sticking-out branch.

As they came to the pine tree, the blue horse came cantering into sight across its field. Martin stopped and gasped in amazement.

"A blue horse!" he exclaimed. "You've got a blue horse."

"Yes," Ruth said.

"You never told me!"

"No," Ruth said, with a slight shrug. "It's not ours."

"Doesn't matter," Martin said. He gazed across the gorse bushes at the incredible animal. "If I had a blue horse I'd never talk about anything else. I'd spend all my time riding on it, far, far away – everywhere! Do you ride him?"

"Not yet," Ruth said. "Some day I will."

"Are you scared?"

Ruth shook her head. "Not scared," she said. "I just don't want to, yet."

They went on along the track, and the blue horse followed them on the other side of the hedge. They passed the signpost where the track split. Martin read out: "'TO SCHOOL; TO THE SEA.' When it's summer-time we'll bring Fuzz up this way and go down to the sea with her. I've done it before – you go through the plantation and the trees stop right at the very edge of the dunes. And we have rides on the sand, and lots of other people come and join in. She likes it. We'd have to start early in the morning, though."

Ruth smiled with pleasure. "We'll have to take a picnic."

Across the gorse bushes, the blue horse snorted.

"The gate's just along here." Ruth pointed.

They went along the track to the gate, and Ruth climbed up onto the second bar, while Martin stood back. The blue horse walked over to her and nuzzled her forehead and hands. But when Martin came forward to the gate, the horse suddenly backed off and stood staring, wide-eyed, stamping its foot and swishing its mist-coloured tail.

"Come on, Blue," Ruth said. She was surprised and a little upset. "This is Martin. He's my friend."

The blue horse reared up violently.

The blue horse stopped swishing its tail and began to look calmer. Martin slowly climbed onto the gate. After a little, he held out his hand towards the horse. "Come on, Blue," he said gently.

The blue horse reared up violently, letting out a half-grunting neigh. Then it shied off and galloped away over the field, sending a spray of muddy turf up behind it.

It was quite unlike anything it had ever done before. Martin looked hurt. His rosy cheeks had gone pale, and after a little while he climbed down from the gate and said, in a flat voice, "He doesn't like me, that's all."

"It must have been something you're wearing," Ruth said. She felt something very queer had happened. She didn't believe that the blue horse didn't like Martin – she didn't believe it was as simple as that. But she couldn't think what the real reason could be.

Ruth thought Martin was offended, but he seemed to get over it quite soon. They went inside by the back door, and Martin stroked all the cats' heads in turn – except for Wattle, who didn't like being stroked. Each cat shut its eyes and opened them again when Martin moved on to the next one. Then Ruth and Martin went out again and amused themselves by rolling large stones down the bank at the edge of the garden and splashing them into the stream. They would have gone on, but Ben went inside and told Ruth's mother what they were doing, and then Ruth was in terrible trouble. It turned out that her father had carried all the stones up from the stream and set them out there in an artistic fashion for his rockery. Ruth told her mother she hadn't known anything about it and her mother said that was because she just never listened. Ruth was ready to go into the sulks, but Martin insisted that they go down to the stream and carry all the stones back up. Ruth helped him with a couple, but then sat down on a rock at the edge of the water.

"I'm fed up," she said. "You're just sucking up to Mum. You don't have to do that."

Martin took no notice. Ruth stared off to the opposite bank, and splashed pebbles into the water beside Martin whenever he came down for another stone.

"We've put all the stones back on the bank," Martin told her mother later, "but I don't think they'll be in the right places."

"Thank you, Martin," Ruth's mother said warmly. "We could do with a helpful lad like you round here more of the time."

"I did it too, you know," said Ruth.

"Martin didn't know they'd been put there in the first place," her mother retorted.

Later, when Martin had gone, Ruth said:

"The blue horse doesn't like Martin. It wouldn't come near him and it ran away."

"And Martin's such a nice boy," her mother said.

"Blue doesn't think so," Ruth answered. But she wasn't sure if that was quite true. Perhaps the horse was just jealous. In fact, when she came to think of it, it had been when they were talking about taking Fuzz down to the sea that she had heard it snorting, across the hedge. How much did the blue horse really understand? It had understood about the sugar, and about her not wanting to ride it yet, but did it really understand about Fuzz? If she had been sure it understood everything – if it could just have spoken to her – it would probably have stayed her best friend and she wouldn't have liked Martin half so much, smarming and charming her mother with his stupid stones.

*Ruth's father covered bits of the garden
with sheets of black plastic.*

Chapter Six

Days and weeks passed. More birds sang every day – blackbirds and thrushes near the house, husky-whistling lapwings and whooping curlews out on the fields. Plants grew taller, trees grew greener. The hedge round the blue horse's field was a mass of yellow gorse flowers and pinky-white may blossom. The shiny-trunked tree that hung over the bank – a laburnum – poured with blossom, like a pyramid hung with bright yellow lambs' tails. The sombre shades of the lone pine tree were almost lost among all the fresh spring colours. The mound where it stood was alive with scampering rabbits.

Ruth's father covered bits of the garden,

including the bank to the stream, with huge sheets of thick black plastic, which he weighted down with the rockery stones. "Now we leave it," he said, "and come the autumn there won't be a weed in sight and we'll be ready to make the perfect rockery." Ruth liked to lie on the black plastic on the bank – it got very warm in the sun – or you could slide down it to the stream...

"Get off that plastic!" her mother screamed from the house. "You'll tear it and then it'll be useless!" Ruth sighed and moved further along, where the bank was wild and grown over with tufty grass and misty blue speedwell flowers.

There came two days when the weather was settled, warm and summer-still. "My dad says it'll stay like this till just before the full moon," said Martin, "so we'll go down to the sea with Fuzz on Saturday."

Arrangements were made. Martin and his father would come up and meet Ruth, and the three of them would go down to the sea together. Ruth's mother would take Ben and the picnic in the car, go the long way round, and meet them down at the beach.

On Thursday evening Ruth went over to the blue horse's field. She had not seen the horse for a fortnight. She hadn't missed it, but she wanted to speak to it now. She didn't know why. She wanted to tell it about going down to the sea with Martin and Fuzz, and she didn't want it to mind, and she wanted to know how much it understood. It would be a test.

She didn't see it at first, so she climbed over the gate and walked into the middle of the field. The grass was much longer than when she had first been there. After a minute she heard the muffled *thud-a-thud* of hooves as the horse trotted up behind her. It was a little queer, because it was coming from the direction of the gate, and she was sure she had looked for it over all that side of the field. She held out her hand and the horse brushed it lightly with the soft hairs round its lips.

"Tomorrow," she said, "no, the day after tomorrow, Martin and Fuzz and I are going down to the sea."

The blue horse's eyes gazed at her, expressionless, lilac-shadowed. Did it understand?

"I'll still like you," Ruth said, "so – so I hope you won't mind." She had been going to say, "I'll still like you the best", but it wouldn't have been true and she didn't want to lie to the blue horse.

She half-expected it would rear up, or buck or shy or something. The thought crossed her mind that it might even lash out – bite her or kick her – and for a moment she felt afraid. But the blue horse did none of these things. It simply stood there, glowing faintly in the evening light, like a horse carved out of blue glass, while its strange eyes gazed at her, and it made no sign, no movement.

"I'm going now," she said, and moved towards the gate. Still the horse didn't move, not even to look round after her as she went. She looked back several times, but it still stood, like a statue, gazing over at the western sky where little clouds floated like tufts of shining golden wool left on a fence.

"That does it then," Ruth thought to herself as she climbed over the gate again. "It doesn't understand – it doesn't understand anything." If the horse had given the slightest sign that it could understand what she was saying, perhaps she might have changed her mind and not gone down to the sea; or she might even have opened the gate and let it come too – a blue horse would surely love to plunge and crash in the blue waves. But it had not understood, so it didn't matter.

The next morning, Ruth woke very early. Her room was glowing with a strange red light. She got out of bed and went to the window. The immense sky was full of crimson clouds. They were hanging so low they seemed just above the top of the laburnum, whose blossoms had turned a dirty orange-pink. The red light seemed to have soaked into everything. The part of the stream she could see from her window glinted sullen red in its narrow valley, like blood.

"Red sky in the morning, shepherd's warning," she muttered. But it couldn't be.

Martin's father had said the weather would remain good till after the weekend. Ruth went back to bed.

When she woke again later the red light was gone, but the sky was grey, overcast with thick, soft clouds. Before she had even got on to the school bus, the rain had started to fall, quiet and fine, but without any sign of stopping.

"You said it wouldn't rain till Monday," she whispered angrily to Martin.

Martin shrugged. "It wasn't me, it was my dad."

"You said he was always right."

"Well, this time he wasn't," Martin snapped.

Ruth suddenly decided she didn't like Martin any more, almost as if the rain was his fault. However, by the time playtime had come she didn't feel so cross. "Perhaps it'll clear up by tomorrow," she said, looking out through the big glass door. The rain was falling in straight sheets, churning up the already deep puddles in the grey playground. The constant, rustling hum of it almost drowned out the thin voices of the playgroup children in the spare classroom.

It poured without pause all that day, and Ruth got soaked on the way home from the school bus, even though her mother came to meet her with a sou'wester and an umbrella. Mixed with the noise of the rain was another noise of rushing water. Just before they bustled in through the back porch, Ruth glanced down the bank to the stream. It was rushing along angrily, brown flecked with creamy foam, and three times as wide as she had ever seen it. It was filling half the width of its little valley, and on its nearer bank it had got under the edge of her father's plastic

The rain was falling in straight sheets.

sheets, which were heaving and billowing like a black tide.

Inside, the floor of the porch was wet with mud and boots, and coats that had been hung up to drip. The only dry thing in it – or rather, the only seven dry things – were the cats, who watched intently from various baskets, boxes and drawers.

Later on Ruth's father went out to look at the stream. "It won't get much higher," he said confidently. "And the stones'll keep the sheets in place."

"Are you sure?" Ruth's mother said.

"The higher the water rises, the wider the channel gets," her father said, "so the more room it has to keep moving. If it keeps moving it can't rise. It's the laws of physics."

Still the rain went on, a monotonous drumming on the roof.

Before she went to bed that night, Ruth

knew that they wouldn't be going to the sea the next day, even if the rain stopped right now. The stream had flooded the track, and all the nearer edge of the blue horse's field was under water.

She slept and dreamed of the sea breaking in huge waves against a rocky shore. But the water wasn't clear, and the waves were brown and angry and their crests foamed and boiled like hot cocoa.

The rain began pouring down again.

Chapter Seven

The rain had stopped next morning, and for a while pale sunlight struggled to get through the steamy clouds.

"You see?" said Ruth's father, "the stream's gone down already. A flood always has its highest point."

Ruth went out in her wellingtons and looked down the bank. She couldn't really see what her father meant, because the water looked to her as deep and urgent and dangerous as ever. At any rate it hadn't washed any of the black sheets away.

But towards lunch-time the sun gave up its struggle and the day became grey again. And over in the direction of the big mountain, land and sky were blotted out in a darkness blacker than any Ruth had ever seen. She hurried indoors.

The darkness deepened, until, not long after lunch, with a sound like an echoing shout from the sky, the rain began pouring down again, pouring as if it would never stop, pouring as if it were angry with itself for having taken a rest that morning. It lashed and crashed, and a wind got up with it, tossing the trees about, sending small birds hurling and whirling through the air, blowing streams of water right across the floor of the porch and under the kitchen door.

Ruth looked down from her bedroom at the tumult outside. Although it was only afternoon, the air was as dark as late evening. Suddenly she gasped and gripped the handle of the window catch, pressing her face against the glass. Down in the rushing water a dark shape was moving up and down, backwards and forwards. The air was so dark, it took Ruth some moments to work out that it was the blue horse. She couldn't tell by its colour because it looked as grey-black as the air, and she couldn't tell by its mane and tail because they looked like the pale flocks of foam in the swirling water. She realized only when it reared up in the water and she saw its hooves shining like red coals in the darkness.

How had it got out? Had its gate been washed away? Was it in trouble? For a little while it looked as though it was struggling and thrashing in the pouring water, being swept on, drowned. Then Ruth saw that this was not so. It wasn't being swept away, but was standing on the steep bank below the garden, and bucking and tossing. It was up to something.

Its glowing-coal hooves were pounding and tearing at the sheets of black plastic. Ruth saw now. It was kicking the stones loose and then tearing free the sheets. She saw one tattered tangle washing loose and tossing and swirling off in the current until it got caught in the branches of the laburnum. And now Ruth noticed for the first time that the old tree had actually fallen. She hadn't seen it coming down, but she could see now that its trunk had sprouted spikes of splintered white wood. It must have come down in the last few minutes. Perhaps, she thought, the blue horse had pushed it down. She couldn't tell what sort of mood the beast was in. It might be angry or it might be crashing about there in the water with a fierce, outrageous happiness. Whichever it was, a tightening feeling in her chest told Ruth that now at last she had begun to be properly afraid of it. Why had it gone for her father's plastic sheets? Why did it want to destroy his rockery? Why did the lovely old laburnum have to be brought down? What would the blue horse do next?

Before she could think what she would do next, she saw her father rushing out of the house in his boots and oilskins. He reached the top of the bank and promptly slipped in the mud. The lower half of him slithered out of sight, and he clawed frantically to pull himself back up. He managed eventually, and then got to his feet and started marching up and down on the muddy grass. Although she couldn't hear him, Ruth could see that he was roaring with fury and disappointment and tearing his hair.

Then further along the bank he managed to grab on to one of the black sheets just as it was being carried off by the water, and for fully a minute Ruth watched in amazement as her father and the blue horse had a furious tug-of-war. The blue horse won. Its hooves ripped the sheet and Ruth's father suddenly sat down holding two handfuls of black plastic while the rest of it went tossing away on the dark water and joined the other sheets tangled in the branches of the fallen tree. Ruth watched her father getting up and walking slowly back to the house, trailing the small black rag of plastic behind him.

He never saw the blue horse, Ruth thought to herself. He can't have seen it. All he's thinking about is the black plastic and his rockery, but if he'd seen the blue horse all he'd have been able to think about would have been the blue horse.

When she looked to see what had happened to the horse, it had gone.

* * *

That night was the worst Ruth could remember. The rain went on and on. The roaring of wind and the rushing of water seemed to shake the house, and the lights began to flicker. Ruth's mother got candles out and started sticking them in holders and jars on various tables and shelves. "Just in case the electricity goes," she said. They tried to watch the television, but it flickered and fizzed and they couldn't get a picture. Even little Ben stopped playing with his toy cars and sat and whimpered.

"It couldn't flood us out, could it?" Ruth's mother said. "Should we lift the carpets?"

"Course not," her father snapped. "Even if it rained all night the water couldn't rise any more."

But Ruth thought he didn't seem as sure as he had before. "Couldn't we take the carpets up just in case?" she said anxiously.

"Didn't you see the blue horse?"
Ruth asked her father.

She hated the thought of their soft new carpets squelching wet.

"No!" her father almost shouted. "Don't you know how much work that is? We'd look pretty stupid if we went through all that and then the water never came near the house."

"Better safe than sorry," her mother said.

"Well – do it if you want then!" he exclaimed. "But don't ask me to help. I'm not tearing up the entire contents of the house on account of a little puddle of water out in the garden."

"Whatever you think," her mother murmured, picking Ben up and starting to get him undressed for bed. "But it's not what I'd call a little puddle."

"Didn't you see the blue horse?" Ruth asked her father.

"Oh, for goodness' sake!" he roared.

"Isn't it bad enough having the worst flood since Noah without you having to bring blue horses into it?"

"It was there," Ruth persisted.

"Oh, was it," her father said. "Well, as far as I'm concerned it can stay there, because if you think, young lady, that I'm rushing out to see if it's cavorting in the water – or perhaps floating along on its back with its sunglasses on – you are mistaken!"

He stormed out of the room and slammed the door behind him, but at that moment the lights went out altogether for a couple of seconds, and then the window burst open and a blast of cold air and a slog of rain came howling in. He came rampaging back, wrestled the window shut – while Ben clung to his mother and screamed – then told Ruth it was her fault for not pushing down the catch properly. Ruth would have argued if she hadn't felt too thankful that the night had been shut out again.

Somehow the lights managed to stay on, though from time to time they flickered alarmingly, and by the time Ruth went to bed the wind had quietened. She stood at her window and strained her eyes out into the darkness. It was still raining, but the night was not completely black. She could make out the huge dark water rushing by, but it didn't seem to have risen to the top of the bank. It had washed away the plastic sheets but it hadn't come into the actual garden. Probably her father was right – it would have been stupid to lift the carpets. As she fell asleep, the sound of the water was almost lulling.

"What's happening? What's happening?"

CHAPTER EIGHT

Somewhere in the dark before dawn, Ruth was wakened by shouts and screams. She leapt out of bed with her heart pounding. She tried to switch the bedroom light on but nothing happened. Ben was screaming, her father was shouting something. He seemed to be downstairs. Her mother, in her pyjamas, clutched at Ruth and held her close against her legs in the strange darkness of the landing. "What's happening? What's happening?" Ruth asked wildly, struggling free from her mother's hold. Her mother was clutching on to Ben as well.

"Don't go downstairs!" her mother squeaked.

"Why? Why not?" Ruth squeaked back, staggering off towards the stairs.

"Ruth!" her mother screamed.

There was a small light waving around in the hall, and strange movement. Ruth peered over the bannister. The light was the small pale beam from a torch, and the movement was big and black and shiny.

The whole of the downstairs was flooded with water, water that was not still but which swirled and eddied.

Splosh, splosh. The beam of light waved nearer and Ruth's father came into view, holding the torch, along with two handfuls of wellingtons, and wading through the water in his dressing-gown. He looked wild and wide-eyed. "I've switched the electricity off at the mains," he gasped, flinging the bundle of boots up to the top of the stairs and then coming up himself.

"Thank goodness for that," Ruth's mother breathed. Then, much more briskly, "Right, you two," she said, "clothes on. Quick as you can. Then your boots."

"What's happening?" said Ruth again, though she could see perfectly well what was happening.

"Come on, quick – no questions," her father said, bustling her back to her bedroom. He fumbled about with his torch until he had found the candle her mother had left there earlier. He took matches from his dressing-gown pocket, lit the candle and then went out, leaving Ruth with the small, surprised-looking flame and its huge shadows.

Everything looked different in that light – like a stranger's bedroom – and as she struggled into her clothes Ruth wondered if she was still the same person who had gone to bed the night before. "How do you know you're not dreaming?" she asked herself as she hauled her jersey on and then had to haul it off again because it was back-to-front and felt all wrong.

When she was dressed she went out to the landing again and got her boots on. She didn't know what they would do next. Would they be leaving their flooded home, driving off into the night in the car? Where would they go? Were other places flooded? Would they have to take the cats? The door to her parents' bedroom was slightly open. She could see her father and mother getting dressed while Ben sat on the bed, with his clothes on and his fists stuck into his eyes, howling. None of them noticed Ruth out on the landing. She sat on the top step of the stairs, peering down into the chilly, rustling hallway.

There was a faint light there now, which she thought must be the light of morning. It wasn't bright, but it was bright enough to see the horrible swirling water that gurgled at the front door and made the telephone table look like an island on stilts – like an oil rig, Ruth thought. Then, with a great swirling of water and a small wave that washed over the top of the lowest stair, the kitchen door opened and the blue horse came into the hall.

It looked large and impossible in that small space, wild and terrible. It shook its mane and sent the telephone table clattering over. The telephone landed – *splash* – upside down and lay helpless, like a drowning beetle, and the blue horse stepped forward and crushed it with its glowing hoof. Ruth saw now that the light was coming from the horse. The water round its ankles shone reddish, but the air around its body was bluish-white, like a misty day in February.

All of a sudden it reared up, sending the shade of the hall light flying off, and brought its hooves crashing down against the living-room door. It pushed its way into the room, and immediately after that there was a sound of ripping. Ruth didn't want to move, but she found herself creeping down the stairs despite herself. The blue horse had torn the curtains down from the windows and was trampling them into the water.

Ruth stood on the lowest step of the stairs and, hanging on by the bannister, leaned out over the water to look properly into the living-room. She had made no sound, but the horse suddenly swung round to face her, knocking an armchair into the television, which tipped backwards, with a great splash, into the water. Ruth watched in horror, and the horse gazed at her with smouldering purple eyes. She felt scared – not exactly of the horse, because she didn't believe it wanted to harm her – but of the damage it could do. She was not sure if it wanted to wreck the house or if it was just being clumsy. "Don't," she said. "Please don't."

The horse took three steps backwards. Its hind foot smashed through the screen of the television, and a small spout of red sparks went up. Then it reared again, scattering a red-lit spume of water about it. A picture flew off the wall and fell spiked on the leg of the upturned chair. Ruth's mother's pot plants got crushed onto the window-sill by the horse's side as it came down again.

Ruth put her hand to her mouth. "Stop," she pleaded. "Stop it, please stop."

The blue horse splashed forward towards her. She pulled herself upright and backed up onto the second step.

The horse came out into the hall again, splintering the telephone table, and turned towards the stairs. Ruth moved up onto the third step.

Suddenly it seemed to her that the horse was going to come up the stairs, and in the same moment she knew that if it came, the flood would come too. She felt angry, desperate, hurt. The horse had been her friend. She had tried to be nice to it. It wasn't her fault that it had never talked to her! Scarcely knowing what she was doing, she leaned forward and lashed out, smacking it hard across the nose. Immediately she wished she hadn't, and backed up another step. But the blue horse didn't flinch, and next moment its forefeet were up onto the first step. The polished wood gleamed redly.

Ruth felt tears tugging at her eyes, sobs tugging at her throat. Tears of anger – tears

The horse was going to come up the stairs.

of sadness. Mostly anger: anger at the horse for making her angry, anger for making her hit it. "Stop it!" she shouted. "Just stop it! Go away! I don't like you!"

The blue horse tossed its head and snorted. Its mane flew around like shining mist. It left a scent like dew on a summer morning – a sweet, sharp, cold scent. Tears welled up in Ruth's eyes and spilled down her cheeks. The blue horse grew blurred. "Please," she whispered, "please. If you go away, I'll never try to go down to the sea. I won't ever ride on Fuzz again."

A silence fell. The water swirling around the floor seemed to grow still. Upstairs, Ben had stopped howling. Ruth blinked.

The blue horse stretched its neck forward till its nose was close to Ruth's face. The velvet-soft nose twitched. Then all at once, as if she had put a shell to her ear, Ruth heard a different sound, a sound that only she could hear – the sound of water, certainly, but distant, soft, the sound of the sea washing endlessly on its shores. And out of that sound, that only she could hear, a soft, high voice – or perhaps only the echo of a voice. She listened, her mouth open, her eyes blank, the flood and all homely things forgotten.

And so the sound faded, and she whispered, half to herself and half to the strange creature there in the hall with her, "Down by the sea? That's where you want me to look for you? Yes – yes, I will, of course I will." And then she blinked, and there was the blue horse quietly backing off the stair, turning, swishing through the still water, into the kitchen and out of sight. The light didn't fade. The dawn had come. A thin sound came through from the kitchen, which Ruth knew must be the yowling of seven upset cats, but which sounded more like the voices of small children singing.

It seemed ages before her mother came and found her standing on the stair, gazing through the kitchen door. Ruth had meant to go back up and tell her parents that she thought the flood would stop now, but she couldn't seem to move. Sadness felt like a weight pressing down onto her shoulders, and she had to prop herself up against the bannister so as not to fall down.

"What on earth's been happening?" her mother said. "Oh – the telephone table – the telephone – the curtains – oh, look at the living-room – oh no, oh dear – oh – oh."

It was all too much. Her mother sank down onto the stairs and started shaking, staring in disbelief at the water gurgling inside the shell of what had been the telephone.

That gave Ruth something else to think about, and she was able to move again. She put her arms round her mother and whispered, "It was the blue horse – but I think it's all right now."

By the time Ruth's father and Ben came to join them on the stairs, almost all of the crushed telephone could be seen. The water was swirling away under the door. By the time everyone had got their boots on and were sloshing about on the sodden carpets, looking in despair at the mess of mud (Ben was especially cross about his favourite red car), the water had gone from the garden and the level of the stream was already halfway down the bank again.

The laburnum lay forlornly.

CHAPTER NINE

They didn't dare switch on the electricity yet, but Ruth's mother boiled water for tea on the gas cooker and made some toast. Ruth went outside while she was doing it. The cats had calmed down, though they looked cross and fluffed-up. "It's not my fault," she told them, but they didn't look as though they believed her.

Outside, the grass was flattened and mud-browned. The laburnum lay forlornly, its splintered trunk sticking up like the horns of a dead antelope, its branches tangled with shattered brown blossom and shredded black plastic. Looking further along the stream, Ruth saw that her pine tree was still standing, but the branch where she had used to sit was broken and trailing on the ground.

Muddy gorse bushes lay on the track outside the blue horse's field, their roots torn up by the flood. The gate lay across the track as well. The water had already drained away from the field, but the grass was full of small, stony channels. Above, the sky was clear, pale blue, as though the rain had washed half its colour away.

They spent a long time over breakfast, still wearing their wellingtons. The blue horse hadn't done any damage in the kitchen, apart from breaking the glass panel and the lock on the back door. Ben had a lovely time making patterns in the mud on the vinyl floor.

"Forget the rockery," Ruth's father said. "It was a stupid idea anyway. There's enough to do in the house getting all this mess cleared up – it'll take months."

"The carpets are ruined," her mother said dully.

"No telly," said Ruth.

"No electricity anyway," her father said.

"Thank goodness it's summertime," her mother said.

"You get summer floods," her father said, "but I've never seen anything like this."

The school had not been flooded, and though people in the village complained about the rainstorm, it had not been half so bad for them as it had been at Ruth's house.

"Wow," said Martin on Monday, "that was some flood. It washed all our ducks away. The geese climbed up onto the straw bales, so they were all right, but Fuzz's roof blew off."

"I don't want to talk to you," Ruth said, turning away.

"What's the matter?" Martin asked.

"I just don't want to talk to you, that's all."

"What have I done?"

Ruth swung round. "It was all your stupid pony's fault. It was all your stupid idea, wanting to go to the sea," she shouted, "and I don't want to see you ever again." She stalked off, leaving Martin gaping after her in astonishment.

The carpets weren't ruined, and there was fine weather and a fresh wind all that week, so that by next weekend things were nearly back to normal.

Ruth went several times that week to the blue horse's field. Someone had put the gate back on, but there was never any sign of the horse itself.

"We'll get a new TV in the autumn," Ruth's mother said. "We can do without one over the summer."

"We'll have a laburnum-wood fire and a ceremonial switching-on of the new TV on the first day of autumn," said her father.

The phone rang. Ruth's mother was on it for a long time.

"What's this about you quarrelling with Martin?" she said afterwards. "Martin's mum says he's very upset."

"Nothing," Ruth snapped, and ran off. She hid and sulked for the rest of that day, but at suppertime her mother asked her about it again. "And don't run off this time," she warned. "Martin's such a nice boy, too."

"He's not," Ruth pouted.

"Well, sometimes we fall out with our friends," her father soothed. "These things happen. But you'll miss being able to ride Fuzz and see all the other animals."

"We used to have animals too," Ruth

flared, "until you got rid of them all."

"Being cheeky isn't going to make things any better," her mother said.

"It was all too much work for us, Ruth," her father said. "Martin's dad doesn't go out to work, and his mother works only part-time, and they don't have a baby like Ben to look after. Try and understand."

Before she went to bed that night, Ruth went out into the back porch and did do her best to understand. Wattle and Blueberry had been lured outside at last by the summer weather. She could see Wattle out on the grass, rolling from side to side on his back and pawing something. "They didn't get rid of all the animals," she told the ten lamp-bright eyes which were fixed on her. "You're still here."

The next day at school, Ruth looked over to

Martin's table. Martin did look sad. "It wasn't really Fuzz's fault," she said to herself. "I rode Fuzz, but I wouldn't ride the blue horse – that's all that was wrong."

"I'm sorry," she said to Martin as soon as she got a chance. "I didn't mean to say those things."

Martin brightened up immediately. "We'll go to the sea the first good day we get," he said.

Ruth thought about this. "I can go down to the sea," she said at length. "Because the blue horse said I had to look for it there. But I promised I wouldn't ride Fuzz again, and it never told me I could."

Martin looked at her very strangely. "Have you been talking to the blue horse?" he asked.

"No," Ruth replied. "I mean – I don't know. I think so. I mean – I think it spoke to me. Once."

Martin never mentioned the blue horse again.

They went down to the sea that summer, not once but many times. Martin rode on Fuzz, who would splash into the shallow water but didn't like the bigger waves much. Other children came and begged for rides as well, but Ruth kept her promise not to ride the pony. She felt it was the least she could do for the blue horse, though something told her that the creature would not come again, not with flood and destruction anyway. It was like Ben having a tantrum, that's all, she told herself, though in fact she knew there was far more to it than that.

Martin's father stood like a cormorant at the edge of the sea, sniffing the tangy breeze and gazing to the endless empty flatness of the horizon. Ruth's mother spread a blanket at the foot of a sand-dune. Ruth was rather shocked to see her smoking one of Martin's father's brown cigarettes as she lay propped against the soft sand.

"Go and have a ride on Fuzz," she said lazily.

"No, I can't," Ruth answered.

"Why not? I'll help you on."

"I just can't, that's all."

"You're so strange," her mother said. "You shouldn't look so wild-eyed and haunted at your age."

Often, down at the edge of the sea, Ruth would catch a glimpse of a wave that, for a second, looked like a horse prancing to the shore. Then her heart would leap, until she saw that it was really only a wave. Or sometimes she would hear a soft whinny among the hissing marram-grass of the dunes, and she would search for an hour at a time, running up and down the sliding sandbanks and calling "Blue! Blue? Are you there?"

But however much she searched, between the windswept edge of the forest and the edge of the sea, Ruth never saw the blue horse again; and even in the sunny stillness between the dunes, she never heard so much as a whisper of the strange, high voice that had spoken to her once.

THE

END

UNDER THE MOON

by Vivian French
illustrated by Chris Fisher

A busy little old woman who cleans cobwebs from the sky; a little boy who is tricked by a wily mother wolf; a sweet apple child and a sour elder bogle... There are three delightful stories in this book – each as bright and magical as the moon itself and ideal for reading aloud.

CARRIE CLIMBS A MOUNTAIN

by June Crebbin
illustrated by Thelma Lambert

Here are five enchanting stories about a small, spirited girl called Carrie and some of the big days in her life – including the day Dad comes home from China, Dressing-up Day at school, and the day Carrie climbs a mountain.

HERE COMES TOD

by Philippa Pearce
illustrated by Adriano Gon

Six eventful read-aloud stories – by the author of
Tom's Midnight Garden – about a lively little
boy called Tod, who receives some special
parcels, is fascinated by an enormous orange,
joins a desperate search, has a visitor, makes a
special birthday present and goes exploring.

"Very simple, easy to read... Well designed with
good black and white illustrations. Lovely
domestic detail. It hits the spot."
Ruth McCarthy, BBC Radio's Treasure Islands

THE STONE MOUSE

by Jenny Nimmo
illustrated by Helen Craig

Elly sees at once that Stone Mouse is special; her brother Ted says he's just a dirty old pebble. But then Ted is angry with everyone and everything – and, as Stone Mouse soon discovers, that means trouble.

"Delightful story... Appealing pictures."
The Irish Times

MORE WALKER PAPERBACKS
For You to Enjoy